My Fairytale Time
Little Red Riding Hood

Miles Kelly

Little Red Riding Hood lived in a cottage by a wood. One day her mother said, "Your Grandma is ill. Please take this basket of cakes and fruit to her."

So Little Red Riding Hood set off with the basket, wearing her red cape. "Don't talk to strangers, especially not to WOLVES!" her mother called.

"Bye Mum!"

Little Red Riding Hood walked through the wood. The trees were tall and made scary shadows. Suddenly, a WOLF JUMPED OUT.

"Hello," growled the wolf.
"Where are you going?"
"I'm taking some cakes and
fruit to my Grandma," said
Little Red Riding Hood.

"What a sweet child you are," said the wolf.
"Why not pick your Grandma some flowers too?"
With that the big bad wolf ran off, leaving Little
Red Riding Hood happily picking flowers.

Little did she know, the
wolf had raced ahead to
Grandma's house.

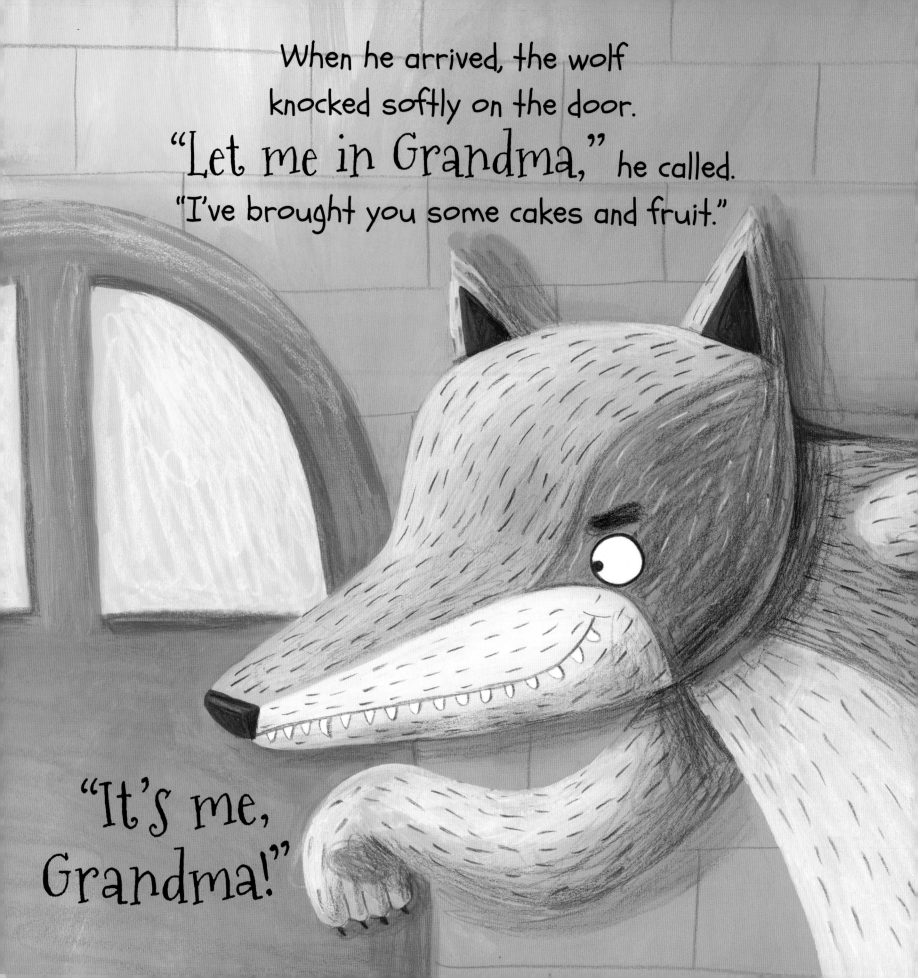

When he arrived, the wolf
knocked softly on the door.
"Let me in Grandma," he called.
"I've brought you some cakes and fruit."

"It's me,
Grandma!"

But Grandma wasn't silly. "That's not Little Red Riding Hood's voice," she said. Quickly, she made her bed and hid in the WARDROBE.

"Grandma?"

The wolf burst into the cottage, but Grandma was nowhere to be seen. So he dressed himself in her nightgown and bedcap and got into bed.

"Grandma, it's me!"

Soon, Little Red Riding Hood knocked on the door. "Come in dear," snarled the wolf in his nicest voice.

"Grandma, you look odd!" said Little Red Riding Hood.

"Come and sit beside me dear," growled the wolf.

Little Red Riding Hood sat on the bed.

"What big ears you have Grandma," she said.

"All the better to hear you with dear," replied the wolf.

"What big eyes you have Grandma."

"All the better to see you with dear."

"And your teeth are just HUGE!" exclaimed Little Red Riding Hood.

"All the better to EAT you with!" said the wolf, and he pounced.

Bang bang
bang!

Little Red Riding Hood **screamed** loudly
and ran away. The wolf leapt after her, but
suddenly there was a banging at the door.

Little Red Riding Hood opened the door. There stood a woodcutter who had heard her screams.

He raised his axe.

With a howl of fear,
the big bad wolf dashed
past the woodcutter, out
of the cottage and away
into the forest.

Then Little Red Riding Hood and the woodcutter heard a strange **knocking** coming from the bedroom.

They opened the
wardrobe door

and out tumbled
Grandma!

"This is a cause for celebration!"

exclaimed Grandma. So she put the
kettle on and laid the table. They all sat
down to tea and cakes.

Yummy!

Never again did Little Red Riding Hood talk to strangers. As for the wolf, he kept well away from little girls – especially those wearing red capes!